A HERO CALLED THE HULK

by Siobhan Ciminera
based on the screenplay by Zak Penn and Edward Norton
illustrated by Dan Panosian

Ready-to-Read

Simon Spotlight
New York   London   Toronto   Sydney

SIMON SPOTLIGHT
An imprint of Simon & Schuster Children's Publishing Division
1230 Avenue of the Americas, New York, New York 10020

The Incredible Hulk, the Movie © 2008 MVL Film Finance LLC. Marvel, The Incredible Hulk,
all character names and their distinctive likenesses: TM & © 2008 Marvel Entertainment, Inc.
and its subsidiaries. All rights reserved.
All rights reserved, including the right of reproduction in whole or in part
in any form.
SIMON SPOTLIGHT, READY-TO-READ, and colophon are registered
trademarks of Simon & Schuster, Inc.

Manufactured in the United States of America
First Edition 10 9 8 7 6 5 4 3 2 1
ISBN-13: 978-1-4169-6053-9
ISBN-10: 1-4169-6053-8

My name is Bruce Banner.

A few years ago I was a scientist.
I worked on many different experiments.

One day something terrible happened.
I was working with gamma radiation.
I wanted to see if it could
make people stronger.
I tested it on myself.

The radiation worked.
I grew strong—too strong!
I turned into a ten-foot monster
that people called The Hulk.
I couldn't control it.
And I hurt many people,
even my friend, Betty.

Because of the gamma radiation,
I turned into The Hulk when my heart rate
went up. I tried very hard to make sure
that never happened.
I didn't want to hurt anyone again.

I moved to Brazil, where I found work
in a factory.
I wanted a simple life.

When I was not at the factory,
I talked to a man named Mr. Blue
on the computer.
We were working together
to find an antidote—something

that would stop me from turning
into The Hulk.

It turned out that the antidote
came from a flower called a *corablanca*
that grew only in Brazil.

I soon ran out of the antidote,
but Mr. Blue had more.
I mailed him some of my blood
so he would be able to give me
more of the antidote I needed.

But before he could help me,
Mr. Blue needed to know more
about my experiment
with gamma radiation.
I returned to the United States
to find my records.
But they had disappeared!

I found the only person I could trust:
my old friend and fellow scientist,
Betty Ross. We had not seen each other
in a long time.

"I need to know more about my experiment, but I can't find any record of it in the lab," I told Betty.

She gave me a data card that contained the information Mr. Blue needed.

I would soon be cured!

Betty also told me where to find Mr. Blue. "His real name is Samuel Sterns," she said. "He's a scientist in New York City."

I had to find Dr. Sterns quickly.
Betty walked me to the bus station.

Suddenly soldiers appeared!
They wanted to capture me,
to find out what the gamma radiation
had done to my body.
But I turned into The Hulk
and escaped with Betty.

I took Betty to a cave where
I knew we would be safe.

I was upset that I had turned
into The Hulk again.

When Betty and I arrived at
Dr. Sterns's lab in New York City,
the doctor put electricity into

my body, and I turned into The Hulk.

Then he gave me the antidote,

and I turned back into Bruce Banner!

"The antidote can't stop The Hulk
from coming out," Dr. Sterns explained.
But he said that the next time
I turned into The Hulk,

I would still feel like myself inside.
This was the best news I had heard
in a long while.

But as Betty and I were about to leave,
soldiers burst into the lab
and took us away.

We were taken to a helicopter and
it was barely in the air when we saw
something happening in the city below.
One of the soldiers in Dr. Sterns's lab
had been injected with my blood.
Now he was a monster
and he was destroying the city!

"I have to go back to help," I said.
I jumped out of the helicopter.
As I fell toward the ground,
I became The Hulk again.
But this time it was different.
I could still feel myself
somewhere inside The Hulk.

The terrible new creature was called
The Abomination.
He was almost as strong as The Hulk.

I did not know if The Hulk
could beat The Abomination.
But The Hulk was ready to fight hard
and not give up.

I realized that day that I am
not a monster.
I can be a hero.
I am The Hulk—The Incredible Hulk!